Jean Pauline
Shares Everything

by Janet Tomita

illustrations by Paul Hart

published by WRITERS PRESS

2

Down syndrome does not
make a broken child.

All the world's children deserve
acceptance, respect, and understanding.
Let us not thrust away those
that only appear broken.

Jean Pauline
Copyright © 1998 by Janet Tomita
Illustrated by Paul Hart
Published by Writers Press

ISBN 1-885101-91-0

10 9 8 7 6 5 4 3 2 1

Printed In The U.S.A.

Dedicated to my niece
Jean Pauline whose
thoughts are always
beautiful.

Janet Tomita

To Lucy–
Keep art in your heart
and keep sharing it
with the world.

Paul Hart

All children have the capacity to share.

Foxtrot Foxy with a bushy, bushy tail,
came to my house carrying a pail.
"Please," said she as she yipped at my door,
"I need to borrow one hot dog
 and maybe two more."

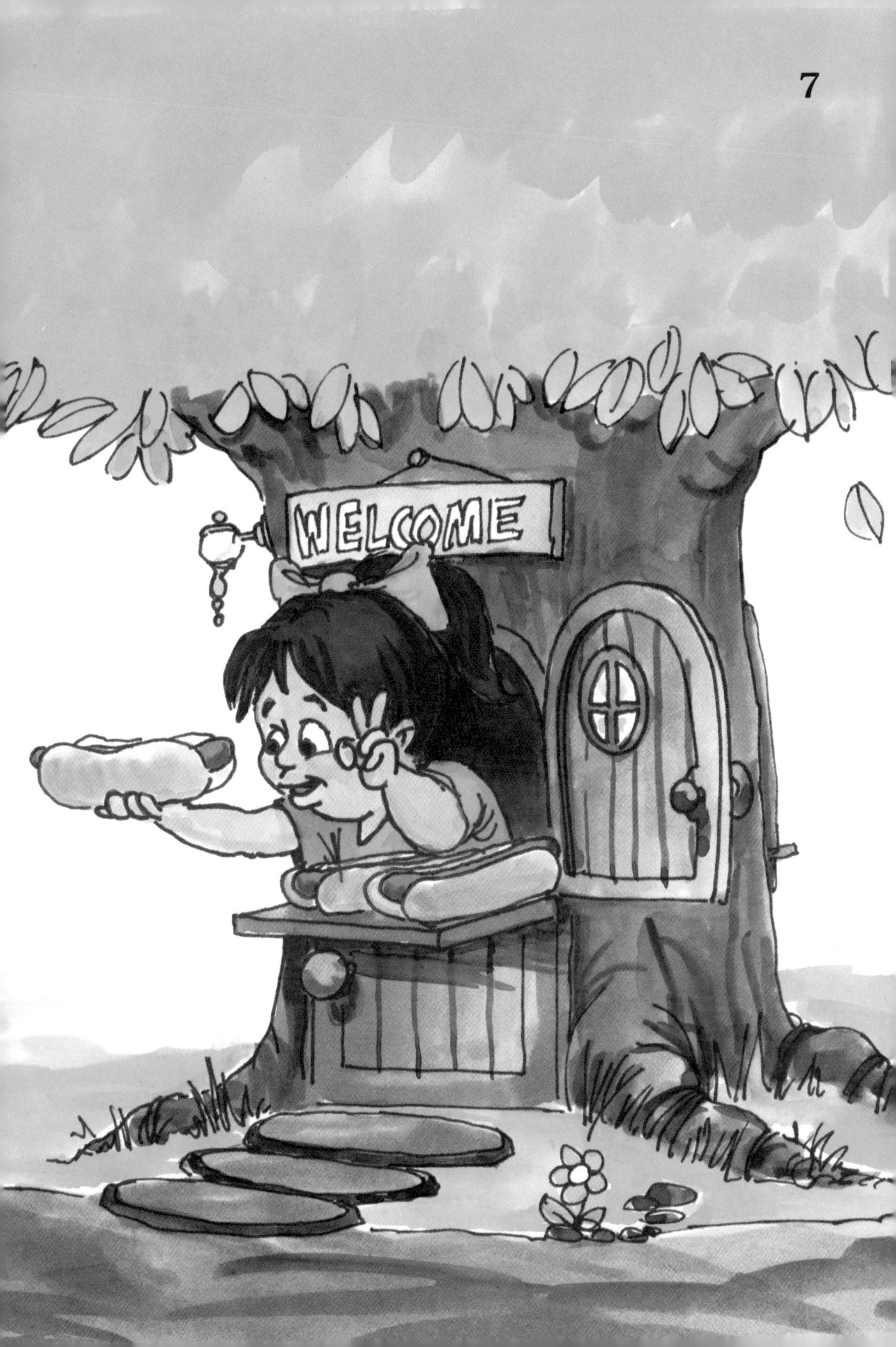
WELCOME

8

Old Annie Ant with her six, six legs,
came to my house pulling an egg.
"Please," said she as she crawled up my door,
"I need to borrow three cookie crumbs
        and maybe four more."

Busy Brown Beaver with his big, big teeth,
came to my house chewing a leaf.
"Please," said he as he slapped at my door,
"I need to borrow five trees
      and maybe six more."

Poky Paul Turtle with his hard, hard shell,
came to my house hauling a bell.
"Please," said he as he scratched at my door,
"I need to borrow seven bugs
        and maybe eight more."

Ring Randy Raccoon with his clean, clean hand
came to my house playing with his band.
"Please," said he as he snooped at my door,
"I need to borrow nine crawdads
        and maybe ten more."

Cranky Chris Moose with his long, long face,
came to my house at a very fast pace.
"I'm sorry," I said as I shut my door,
"all my things are gone
          and I have no more!"

Then Itty Bitty Lady Bug with her
spotted, spotted back,
flew into my house with a black knap sack.

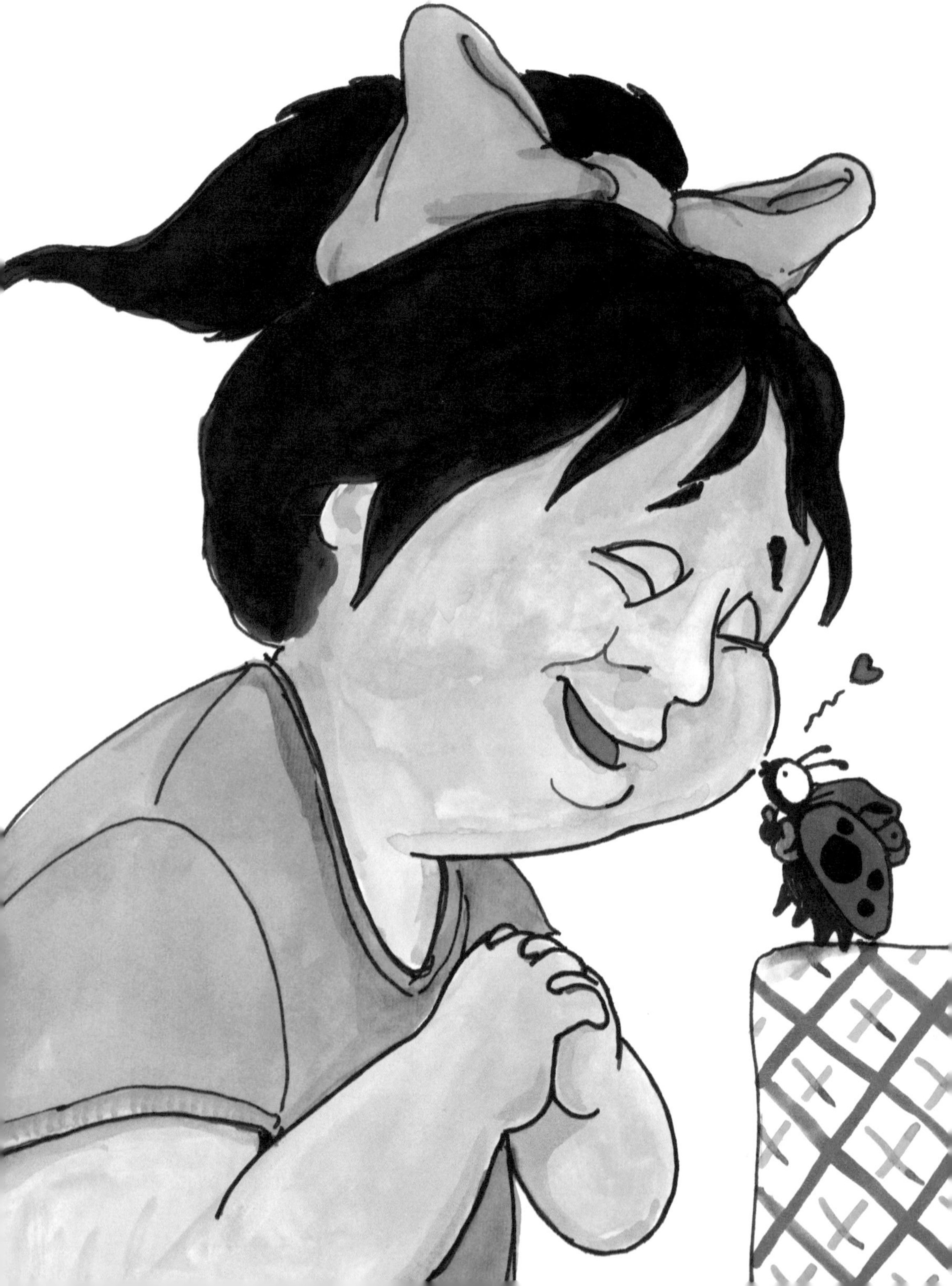

"Please," said she, "hold still little miss,
you've been so kind so here's a big kiss!"

Jean Pauline with her sweet, sweet smile,
saw her friends put her things in a pile.
"Thank you," they said, "for sharing, lovely lass
Foxy even brought,
    the hot dogs under glass.

More great children's books that include ALL children!

—— Enrichment Collection Set #2 ——

Becca & Sue Make Two by Sandra Haines
With practice and cooperation, *together we're better.*
Donnie Makes A Difference by Sandra Haines
Perseverance wins in this inspirational story.
My Friend Emily by Susanne Swanson
Helping through friendship and understanding.
Lee's Tough Time Rhyme by Susanne Swanson
Preparation conquers challenges.
The Boy on the Bus by Diana Loski
Understanding teaches lessons in friendship.
Dinosaur Hill by Diana Loski
Adventure without limitations.
Zack Attacks by Diana Loski
Success in spite of adversity.

—— Other inclusion-minded books ——

Eagle Feather
by Sonia Gardner, illustrated by James Spurlock
A *special edition* treasure of Native American values in stunning artwork.
Catch a Poetic Hodgepodge
by Kevin Boos, illustrated by Paul Hart
A whimsical collection of poems especially written for children.

1-800-574-1715
www.writerspress.com

WRITERS PRESS

5278 CHINDEN BLVD.
GARDEN CITY, ID 83714